Evil Crown

By: Anna G Berry

Chapter One

What bullshit is this? My blood whore lasted only a few minutes. Fuck! My mother and father won't like the fact that I will need another one once again. It is not my fault that theses damn humans make me want to drain them dry because they do not know how to act. They think they can run away, and I cannot stand that shit. Oh, let me tell you who I am. I guess you'd like to know who is telling this damn story.

The name is Damon Silverman. I am twenty-six years old, and I come from a long line of powerful and old vampires. You see, I am heir to the throne of my clan. I have eleven brothers and sisters, but I am the oldest. I do have a twin sister who is happy that I will have the throne. Do I want the throne? Yes, I do but my people think that I am not ready for it. They say that I have a temper and that I party too much. They also say that I screw anything that has a female part.

I smoke too much and drink too much to be ready to take over when my mother and father are done. I have also been told that I should find my mate before I take over as well. I do not need a fucking mate and no female is capable of handling me. I do not like when a woman tells me what to do, expect for my mother and my sisters. Family is one thing, but other females is something different.

I let the human girl drop to the floor, she did not taste good at all. Her blood felt dirty and stale. When that happens, it makes me sick. I grabbed my phone and texted my brother.

Me: Where was my blood whore from?

Rafael: The guards got her from a bar in Hollywood. Why?

Me: She tasted dirty and stale. I'll have to find my own slave then if they keep this shit up.

Rafael: Do you want me to come with you or have Luke go with you?

Me: Both of you can come with me if you want.

Rafael: Okay sounds good.

Me: Meet me outside in five.

I placed my phone on the bed and headed to the shower. I knew my brother and cousin would bring me to some college party filled with humans. I on the other hand like fae parties, they know how to through them. I shook my head as I got out of jeans and boxers and stepped in the hot shower water. I stood there for a few seconds letting the water wet me everywhere. I then began to wash my body before getting out. I wrapped the towel around my waist and walked to my closet. I grabbed a black shirt, black jeans, and black shoes. I got dressed and headed toward the stairs. I closed the door and made my way down to the front door.

"Where are you going?" I heard my mother's sweet voice ask me as I got the door.

"I'm going out with Rafael and Luke; I'll behave or try to at least," I told her as I gave her a kiss on the cheek before opening the door.

She gave me a nod and turned away toward the reading room. I smiled and walked out the door, letting it close behind me. I walked to a 2019 black BMW i8, I got in the back and Luke took off toward Malibu. For us it took about three minutes but for any human it would have taken about two days. You see where my soon to be kingdom is, it's in Malibu but it's on a different plane all to itself. For a human to find it themselves would be extremely hard. We made it that way just so if a human got out and tried to make it back to their world it would be a long road back and we could easily get to them. May sound cruel but fuck it. I like to hunt them before I kill them it makes for great fun. I like to have my prey fear me; I get off on it. Hell, just thinking about it is making me go crazy.

"Alright, we are here," Luke said as he pulled me from my thoughts.

I got out and looked around, sure enough we were at a college party. I gave Luke my 'why am I here?' look before following him into the party. I love my cousin like he was one of my brothers but sometimes he makes me want to kill him. I follow him to a group of girls. Out of now where I get a strong pull toward the girl that is wrapped up in Luke's arms. I shook my head and thought that I should be friendly and began to make my way around the party.

The college girls were all drunk and making out with the guys. I made my way to the back yard and found a group of girls that did not have a male in the mix. I walked up to them and gave them a smile. They all let out a giggle and began to stumble over their words.

"How are you ladies tonight?" I asked as I could smell their blood making my mouth water.

"Good," they said in unison.

I walked to each one and smelled them, letting my hunger decided on who will be my next blood whore. I was hoping that one of them would not try to do anything fucking stupid. I kept getting pulled to the girl that Luke had on his arm. Something about her was making me crave her and her blood. I gave the girls a smile before walking back inside. I began to feel overwhelmed; I took a deep breath. I walked over to Rafael and Luke.

"I need to go home," I told them as I ran my figures through my hair.

"You, okay?" Rafael asked.

"Not fucking sure but I need to go." I looked around to see the girl walking back toward us.

She walked up and gave all of us a smile, she opened her mouth to speak but I didn't hear anything. I shook my head and tried to speak but I couldn't say anything to her. This is fucking bullshit; I want to speak to her and ask her why she's making me go fucking insane. I let out a deep breath and felt myself walk to the front door.

I then heard a scream, and my nose was filled with the smell of blood. It snapped me out of this trance. I looked back to see a guy with a large cut on his forearm. I walk back over and pulled out my phone.

"What happened?" I asked the crowd.

"He dropped his bottle and it shattered, then he tried to pick it up and he cut himself," a girl shrieked.

"Okay, I need someone to get a towel and apply pressure to the area. The rest of you please go outside while the EMTs are here." I called out orders while I dialed for an ambulance.

Luke came with a towel and gave it to the girl. She began to talk to the guy as she applied pressure. I couldn't help but stare at her. The pull I was feeling got stronger and stronger by the minute. I could tell she felt it too, she couldn't help but look at me. I looked at Luke and Rafael nudging my head toward the door. They gave me a nod and we headed to the front door. I needed to be away from the blood and her as much as possible. We got outside and it felt like I could breathe again.

"What's going on Damon?" Luke asked.

"One, the blood was making me hungry and two who is that girl?" I let out a growl as I couldn't help it.

"Her name is Anabella; she goes to school here." Luke looked confused by my behavior and in fact I was too.

I gave him a nod; I knew that my behavior was strange. I don't act that way in front of a large group of people. I began to pace as I could still smell her. I knew I had to tell them what was going on.

"Is she human? She smells non-human almost vampire like us. Her scent is driving me crazy, and I don't know what to do." I growled again.

"I'm not sure, when I first met her, she seemed to be human but now I'm not sure. She does everything a human dose expect she doesn't smell like one," Luke said, a bit in shock by realizing what I said.

"Do you know her last name?" I asked.

"Actually, I do. Its Dracul, Anabella Dracul. Why?" he cocked his head to the side.

"It's for research later," I told them as I typed her name in my phone.

I looked up to see that the ambulance had pulled up and were making their way to us. I gave them a smile and walked to the front door. I opened it and showed them where the guy was laying. The blood had slowed down a lot and the

EMTs began to work on the deep cut before having him get into the back of the vehicle. Once they took off, I walked to the back yard.

"Everyone is free to come inside now. The EMTs just left with the guy." I told everyone as I held the door open.

They all began to walk inside and began to party again. I shook my head as I couldn't understand humans. I mean I love to fuckin party, but this shit is stale as hell. I walked back outside to find the boys walking to the car.

"What's going on?" I asked as I got to it.

"Mom wants us home for some reason," Rafael said giving out a deep breath.

I gave a nod and got into the car. We pulled out the driveway and began to go home. It took us about three minutes and we were through the plane back to the mansion. Luke parked the car in front of the house as we all got out. We all looked at each other and gave a nod before opening the door to see what my mother wanted.

To our surprise it was my father and my uncle waiting for us. They didn't say anything but turned around and walked into the meeting hall.

This should be fun. I hate meetings but it's part of being a future king, I guess. We walk in to find the hall filled with other clan kings. Great, just what I need more people to tell me that I need to fucking change my ways. You know what, screw them. What I really need to do is research that girl and find out why she was driving my fucking crazy.

"Good to see you Prince Damon, Prince Rafael and Prince Luke," King Graw of Ireland said.

All three of us bowed and took our seats. We all knew that we weren't getting out of this meeting. I took a deep breath and gave everyone a nod. I wasn't sure what the fuck it was about, but my mind wasn't here anyway. They were talking about political things that I nodded at when I was spoken to but that was it. Then I heard of the lost and forgotten kingdom in

Washington state. I heard that the family was wiped out. I sat up in my chair as I heard them talk.

"What happened to the clan?" I asked now very intrigued.

"They got wiped out and all family became mortal at least the daughter was," King Hall of the east coast said.

"Why? What did they do to deserve that?" I wanted to know, I felt that Anabella was a part of it, but I could be wrong.

They looked over at me. I gave them all a look that I really wanted to know. My father gave them a nod. Hell, if I'm going to be king, I needed to know everything that has happened and why it did. I got more comfortable in my seat and waited for one of the other kings to answer my question. To my surprise it was my father who spoke up.

"They didn't actually do anything. The king was a very good friend of mine. He wasn't wiped out per se. He got banished from his kingdom and was to walk in the mortal world until he regained our trust. He was a suspect in a human's death that the humans had video of. He swore he did not do it, that he was being framed for it. We had a meeting and decided to spare him and his family. His wife died shortly after, and he was left with a daughter to care for. It is said that she was mortal and has showed no aspects of being a vampire. We always keep an eye on them, it makes it safer that way." My father seemed hurt after he was done telling it.

"So why say that they were killed?" I was confused by the information.

"It's easier for us to tell everyone that," my uncle said as he gave me a small smile.

"Ah, I see. Are the records destroyed or are they still available for us to read? I want to get to know all the kingdoms even the ones that aren't here. As future King I have a right to them." I looked around the room to see that they all nodded to tell me that the records were still available.

"Are we done? I have some work to do." I leaned back in my chair.

"What exactly is that?" asked King Stone of the north.

"Research on the kingdoms so I can get to know everything before I become king." I gave him a fuck off look before getting up and walking toward the door.

"I'll be in the library if anyone needs me." I looked back and walked out of the room.

Chapter Two

I walked into the library and took a deep breath. What the hell was that meeting about anyway? I ran my hands through my hair and shook my head. I was getting ready to head to the kingdoms records room when I heard the door open. I turned around to see Rafael and Luke walking in. I let out a chuckle, these assholes were going to need to learn to leave me alone.

"So how did you both get away from the meeting so fast?" I asked suppressing a chuckle.

"We just walked out, father and uncle weren't really surprised by it and didn't stop us," Rafael said as he gave me a shrug.

I let out a husky laugh and turned around toward the records room. I could feel both of them following me as we made it to the door. The door was an old antique, it was round and made out of Cherry wood. It had to be as old as the house, it was a weird shape for the house. I looked at the door handle to see it was an odd shape. It was a male loin's head with a huge ancient metal ring hanging out of its mouth. I looked at Luke and Rafael before looking back at the door. They both shrugged their shoulders and gave me a nod.

I reached over to it and gave it a pull. It did not budge, I looked over to see there was a strange lock on it. I looked around the door for the key but couldn't find it. I turned around to see the desk in the middle of the room. I walked over and began looking on top of it but still could not find the damn thing. I let out a deep sigh and reached for the top desk drawer. It opened and on top of a book was the key. I grabbed the book and the key. I walked back to the door and placed the key into the lock. It clicked as I turned the key, the lock opened, and I softly pulled it off the door.

I placed the lock on the nearby table, I gave the door another tug and this time it opened with ease. I heard it creak open and was a bit stiff like it hadn't been open in centuries. As soon as it was all opened, dust and cobwebs where all over the place. I took a step in and reached for the light switch, but I couldn't find it at first. I let my eyes adjust to the darkness—perks to being a vampire we can see in the dark. It didn't take any time at all to see that there was a light switch on the back wall. I walked over and flipped it on, and it lit the whole room up. It sure looked like no one had been here. I walked over to the left side of the room, I figured to start from left to right. When I walked over there, I found it was my family. I moved to the next aisle to see that it was Luke and his family, you may think why my family and his are not together. My uncle and my father are bothers but my uncle married my aunt the only heir to her family throne, so he married her and rules over her clan.

I went to the next one to find the Graw family and pulled out the family tree. I wanted to cover every other family before I go find the banished king. There was a big round table by the big stained-glass window where the light switch was. I put the book on it and dust came off the table in a giant cloud. All three of us let out coughs as we waved the dust away. As soon as the dust settled and went away, I opened the book, and I heard the binding crack. Dust seemed to fly out as well. I waved the dust away again. I flipped through until I found a picture of the family tree.

As I ran my eyes through the paper, I didn't see anyone that was marked out or Anabella listed on the page. I closed the book and thought that it disappeared when the king was banished. There might be a book on him, there are several of my uncle in my family's bookshelf. As I scanned the shelves, I couldn't find anything.

"Luke, Rafael, help me look for that king on Graw's shelf." I looked over at them.

They gave me a nod and walked over to the bookshelves. I knew we weren't going to go through the whole room in one day. I planned on looking at one family at a time. It made it easier to take my time and not miss anything. I looked at every book we all thought could have something in it. We placed every book on the table and combed through each to find nothing that raised my eyebrows. I let out a deep breath. This was getting really fucking aggravating, there was no mention of this king at all.

I shook my head and ran my figures through my hair. I looked at my watch to see that it was getting late. I knew all of us were getting tried and needed to get some sleep. I walked over and turned off the light to the room.

"Come on, we can come back, or I'll come back later. I know you two must be tried and want to get some sleep," I tell them as I walked to the door.

"We can defiantly help you look tomorrow too," Rafael said as I closed the door and locked it back up. I placed the key and the book that was in the desk in my pocket.

We all walked out the library and I closed the door. I gave them a nod and made my way to the main stairs. I saw that my mother's reading room light was still on. She's normally not up right now. I walked over to make sure everything was okay. I peeked in to see that she was reading a book.

"You're still up?" I asked a bit confused.

"Oh, I didn't realize the time. Your father is probably wondering where I'm at." She looked up from the book and placed it on her table next to her chair.

"Go get some sleep, you need it more than me anyway," I told her as I held my hand out for her to take it.

She grabbed my hand and stood up, brushed off her dress and smoothed it out before giving me a smile. She let go and made her way up the stairs. My mother was very beautiful and graceful. No wonder my father went after her, she was second in line for my uncle's kingdom. My father had two others that were just as beautiful and were into him but with us we have mates. He was crazy about her; she was as well but gave my father a run for his money. It took four times for my father to propose to her for her to say yes. He never gave up on her. One day I hope to finally agree to settle down and wish to find someone the way my parents did. Then again, I doubt there is a woman out there that can tame me as what everyone says.

I shook my head and walked up the grand staircase. My room was on the third floor on the left, third door. It had the best view of the back left side of the yard. It was the go-to for all the slaves that like to think they can fuckin' escape this place. I let out a husky laugh and opened my bedroom door. My room was big, some would say that it was huge. The bed was a California King, and it was a four-poster made out of mahogany. There was a door to the left that was meant for slaves. A few inches away was a wardrobe and a vanity as well. Right in front of the bed against the other wall was a black sofa. To the right of that was the bathroom, to the left of the sofa was a nice size glass door that led to a balcony.

I looked around and smiled, I love that my room is so dark. The walls are painted black, and the window curtains are a deep dark red. Even my bed sheets are a dark red. I walked toward the bathroom; I needed a shower, and it might help me with sleeping. I turned on the water and undressed, I checked the water temperature. It was perfect, just the way I liked it. Hot almost burning hot. I stepped in and let the water coat my whole body. I closed my eyes, it felt fucking amazing. I opened them and began to wash my body and hair. As I turned off the water, I reached for the towel that was on the hook outside of the shower.

I warped the towel around me and walked to the sink. I brushed my hair and began to brush my teeth; the fangs need to be kept clean or the blood will taste fucking weird from the next blood whore. Blood whores are what we call humans who are willing to give their blood to us. I smiled at my reflection and saw that my fangs where fresh and clean. I let out a yawn and walked over to my bed.

As soon as I got to the edge of the bed, I laid down and fell fast asleep. The sleep was not what I expect. I get pulled into a very odd dream, like one I didn't want to wake up from. I wanted to see what was going on until the end.

I was at a frat party with Luke, I was standing next to him and a group of guys. The party's music was loud, but it wasn't shaking the walls. There was also smoke covering the rooms as well. I couldn't help but take a deep breath, I inhaled the smoke to find that it was weed smell. I didn't mind the smell as fae smoke as well. I walked toward the back of the house to see that the yard was filled with humans. What the fuck is going on? I rubbed my face and shook my head. I walked back toward the front of the house, I heard Luke calling my name. As I got up to the front, I heard a female's voice calling my

The next thing I knew, I woke up. "What the fuck was that?" I sat up in the bed.

I looked at the window and saw that it was the afternoon. Maybe some fresh air and a walk around the rose garden. I got out of the bed to find that I had fallen asleep naked, I must have fell in the bed with just the towel on. I let out a laugh and walked over to the closet that was next to the wardrobe. I walked in and grabbed a white button shirt, black dress pants, I grabbed my dress shoes. I felt like I needed to wear this shit. I got dressed and grabbed my jewelry, I placed my chain necklace on. I grabbed the rings and slid them on my fingers, I most definitely made sure to put my emerald ring on, it helped me not burn up from the sun. Every person in my family had a different color stone, Rafael has blue Sapphire. One has black Onyx, one has Ruby, and another one has Topaz. That was to name a few. The males wear rings and the females where a beautiful choker. The slaves even have their master's stone too, so a female human would wear the choker and a male human would wear a bracelet instead of the ring like we wear. That's how we track them and know when they try to escape. Our ring or choker would begin to vibrate when the slave got to a certain point of our land.

I opened the door and walked down the stairs, I walked down to the feed room. I stood at the door and froze. It was like I couldn't go in; I was starving. I shook my head and opened the door. I needed to eat, I walked over to the woman who I didn't care to learn her name. She let out a giggle and began to blush.

"Good to see you again Prince," she said as she held out her wrist.

"Yeah," I told her before sinking my fangs into her skin.

She let out a moan and she laid still; I felt her body begin to heat up. I took my left hand and ran it up her right thigh. She let out another moan and begged me to do more. Most female humans do, so I let my hand find that sweet fuckin' pussy. She was so wet; I could smell her wetness mixed with her blood. I slipped my fingers in and teased that sweet pussy of hers. She began to wiggle, and I dug my fangs in deeper. She obeyed; I love when I can make a woman feel good. I picked up speed and she came as soon as I pulled my fangs out.

"That's a good girl, now I have work to do and I will see you soon." I gave her a wink as she shook her head.

Chapter Three

I walked out of the feed room and toward the back of the house. The rose garden was at the back of the house, and it was my favorite place to be alone. Fuck, it's the only place that I love to be alone. I looked into the kitchen to see that they were making dinner for tonight. I got to the door and saw that my father was outside sitting in one of the chairs with a glass in his hand. I opened the door and walked over to him.

"What's going on?" I asked.

"Thinking of handing the throne over to you sooner but not sure you are ready for it," he told me as he took a sip of his glass.

"I'm fuckin' ready for it, and I'll prove it." I gave him a nod.

"Prove it then," was the only thing that he said.

I gave him another nod and walked over to the garden. Great now he doesn't think that I'm ready for it. What the hell? I knew that the rest of the kings didn't think that I'm ready but my father? Well, I guess I have to show them that I'm ready for it then. I took a deep breath and walked over to the bench in the middle of the garden. I sat down and looked around, I could see the sun was slowly fading and the sky got dark. I closed my eyes, hoping to figure out what the fuck to do next. Well, I kept seeing her, I shook my head and opened them. I got up and walked around the garden. I felt my feet heading to the graves, I didn't know why I was going there. I stopped at my great grandfather's grave; I really do miss him. Everyone kept saying that I was a lot like him. I couldn't believe it but at the same time I did. Everyone said that he played around with a lot of women before he met my grandmother.

"Wish you were here. Everyone thinks I'm not fucking ready to be king. What would you do?" I took a deep breath and rubbed my face.

"Follow that damn heart of yours, stop fuckin' around. Stop being like me," I heard my grandfather's voice.

I looked around to see where the voice was coming from but couldn't find anything.

I shook my head, "I don't know how. There's this girl that keeps showing up in my dreams, do I keep reaching out towards her?" asked him.

"Do your research, it will help you get to know the kingdoms and the girl," he told me.

"Is the girl like us?" I asked him.

"That is for you to find out." His voice drifted off.

I took a deep breath as he faded away. I turned around and headed back to the house. I knew that dinner was ready and that they would be looking for me. I would eat then go to the library and continue with the research on a new clan. I stopped at the garden and smelled a few. I decided to use my speed and got the back door. I don't usually use it unless I really need too but I was feeling a bit lazy. I walked into the dining hall and saw that not everyone was there. I took my seat and waited for everyone to take heirs.

Everyone was a bit too quiet. "What's going on?" I asked breaking the silence over dessert.

"Nothing is going on." My father was very short with the answer.

"Something's fuckin' going on. Why the hell is everyone so god damn quiet?" I couldn't help but get annoyed.

"Fine, we got something in the mail that can change everything," he said pulling something out of his pocket.

"Well, what is it?" I grabbed the envelope to find it was a letter to me.

I opened it to see it read,

Dear Prince Damon,

I'm writing to you because it's sad to inform you that you can only take the throne by finding your mate and Queen. Until then you are not allowed to ascend the throne.

Very respectful,

The clan council.

I looked up to see that the whole room was looking at me. I shook my head, unfuckin' believable. I balled up the letter and felt my anger begin to boil up. I got up and shot to the library. I could hear my mother calling my name and I needed to find this girl before I tore this state apart looking for her. I could feel Rafael on my heels, I was actually glad he followed in. I needed all the help I could get to find her. I threw the door to the library open, I ran toward the records room and unlocked it. The door opened and I ran to where I left off.

I pulled King Hall's family tree book out and placed it on the table. I flipped open the book and begin to look for the picture of the tree. When I got the tree, I began to scan the page to find her or the lost king. I slammed the book shut and placed it back on the shelf. I scanned the shelves to find anything on her even if it was about her father. I tore every book apart and still couldn't find her. I went to the next shelves.

This time it was King Black, he had a long list of family in his tree. I held out hope to find something on them. As I used my eyes to scan the pages, I stopped on a name that had her last name.

"Hey, Rafael. Come look at this." I called him over and pointed at the name.

"That's the last name that Luke told us. Let me look to see if they have any books on that name." He jogged over to the bookshelf.

I gave him a nod and flipped in the family book, I found only a page that was filled with his picture and a small paragraph of him. It only had his date of birth which was 300 B.C. No date of death. It had where he was born, which was Greece, and it also said that he was married but nothing about his children. I closed the book and placed it back on the shelf. Rafael was able to find three books on him. I also asked him to see if he could find his own section. I placed the books on the table and opened the first one.

It had all of his war history, nothing on his family. I closed the book and opened the second one. The second on didn't have anything about his family either, it was all about him, ended when he married his wife. I ran my fingers through my hair and closed the book. I opened the last one and it seemed promising, it had the post marriage. It actually had a few pages that mentioned a pregnancy and a child.

There was no name of the child, I read the whole thing and still couldn't find a thing on the name. I took a deep breath; this wasn't helping anything.

"The room is huge, and it would take me all night and day to find it," Rafael said as he walked back.

I gave him a nod, "We look later but for now let's look into this book for what we can find." I sat down in one of the chairs.

He gave me a nod; he took a seat across from me. I slid the book to the middle of the table. I scanned the table to see that there was a notebook. I grabbed it and opened it up. To my surprise there wasn't anything written in it. I pulled it closer and grabbed a nearby pen so we could take notes on it. As we began to look more into the book the pages seemed to fade away from it. We both looked up at each other very confused, we both looked down and flipped more through the book. The more we went through it the more the pages began to fade and become just the raw paper.

I looked down at the notebook that I was trying to make notes on and found that it looked like I didn't write anything on it at all. I was confused as hell, and I could tell Rafael was just as pissed as I was. I took a deep breath before my temper rose. I picked up the book, I closed it and then opened it up again. I found that the words were back, and it was filled with information. I set it down and began to take notes. Again, the words started to fade, and the pages began to get darker. I closed it and looked on the back cover. I found nothing that could tell me as to why it was doing this.

I shook my head and stood up, I walked over to the bookshelf of King Black. I placed back on the shelf and walked back to the table. As I looked at the notebook it still was blank. How the fuck is it blank? I ran my figures through my hair before pacing back and forth. I walked toward the window, and as I looked out of it, I saw that it was pouring down raining. I looked up at the sky, doubting myself confidence about being a king.

Also, how the hell am I going to find my mate? What, they think that she will just fall out of the fucking sky? I let out a growl that has been waiting to come out since I got that damn letter. Can they really do that? My father seemed to think that they can. I need to get out of this damn house. I looked over to Rafael to see him on his phone.

"Want to get out for a bit?" I asked as I walked over to him.

"Sure, where are we going?" He clicked his phone to lock it.

"Not sure, we can drive around this realm or the human one for a while?" I suggested.

"Okay, want me to drive?" He stood up and placed his phone in his pocket.

"Yeah, that will work. I just need to get out and get some air to think about what to do next," I told him as I walked toward the door.

We headed out of the record's room and out of the library. I couldn't help but feel like taking the tunnel to the garage. I tugged on Rafael's arm and motioned him toward the tunnels. The tunnels started right by the library, there was a door a few feet from it. It led to underground tunnels that went all over the house, a lot of them came out to our rooms and to the garage. I opened the door and Rafael went in first then I closed the door behind me. The tunnel that led out to the garage was a bit confusing if you didn't know where you were going.

We headed straight for about four hundred feet then we turned right. We walked down that tunnel for about six hundred feet and then turned left. As we walked about another six hundred feet there was fork in the tunnels. I looked over at Rafael to see if he remembered if we go left or right, he shrugged his shoulders and walked toward the right. I shook my head but followed him anyway. To my surprise he picked the right way. We came to a door at the end of the tunnel. I opened it to see that it was in fact the garage. I let out a deep breath that I must have been holding in since Rafael picked the way.

We walked over to his car, which was a 2020 matte olive-green Chevrolet Camaro. He unlocked it causing it to start and we got in. He opened the garage door and we pulled out. I didn't tell him where to go but he figured it out by my body language. We made our way to a local bar, he thought I could use a drink and maybe take a girl home for the night. I sure the hell needed to get laid soon. Not getting laid and also having pressure to find my mate so I can be king was getting to me. I needed to let off some steam one way or another.

We pulled up to the bar and found a nice spot to park, we then got out and headed in. It wasn't that crowed, which I was very surprised by how open it was. We walked up to the bar and ordered our first set of drinks. I got an Old Fashioned and Rafael got some girly drink, I think it was a Cucumber Sunrise. I have no idea what the fuck is wrong with my brother. We walked over to a table in the center of the room to check out who comes into the bar. I looked around to see that it was mostly males, from vampires, fae, wizards just to name a few.

I looked back at the door to see a smoking hot female vampire walk toward the bar. She ordered a Sex on the Beach. What the hell is with all these drink names? I followed her until she knew I was watching her. She looked at me and smiled. I waved my hand for her to join us. She smiled brightly and she walked over.

"Hello, sweetheart. How are you doing this evening?" I asked sweetly.

"Hi, I'm doing great. Want to get out of here?" she asked both of us.

I looked at Rafael who shook his head yes, he wanted to get laid as much as I did. We shared a lot of chicks and even had sex at the same time with one. It was a lot of fun. He licked his lips and slapped her ass as she took a sip of her drink.

"Yeah, let's get out of here sweet thing," we both told her as we finished our drinks.

Chapter Four

We walk out to the car and slid in; she didn't climb into the back like most do. She in fact sat at my feet. She undid my pants before I could get comfortable in my seat. She managed to get my pants down before I could realize what she was doing. I looked down to see that she had my cock in her hands warming it and getting it nice and hard. I couldn't help but let out a long moan as I laid my head back on the set. Then she put all of it in her mouth, I was very surprised that she took it all. Most can't take all of me, she began to roll her tongue around and began to suck it like a lollipop.

I let out a moan. "Fuck, this is fucking awesome."

She looked up and gave me a smile. She then began to suck faster causing her to choke on my cock. I smiled and grabbed her hair, I held her head in place as she choked on it but kept on sucking it. I then grabbed her head and began letting her head bob back and forward. Her eyes rolled in the back of her head as she took all of it very fast. I let out a smile as I knew she couldn't keep up. I knew she wanted to come up, but she made a bad mistake starting off with me. You start to blow me off, I'm going to finish my load in that fucking mouth of yours. I could feel myself start to cum. I held her head in one spot and arched my body so that all of my cock was fully in her mouth when I came. She wasn't ready and had some of my cum on her corners of her mouth.

"Swallow it, or I will give you a fucking punishment when we get into that room," I growled at her.

She nodded her head and swallowed my cum. I let go of her head and she let my cock slip out of her mouth. She licked the corners of her mouth, and she was out of breath. Well, she's about to be out of breath a lot tonight with us. I let out a chuckle and gave her a wink.

We got back to the house, we made it into Rafael's room as no one questions when he brings a girl home. He grabbed her and threw her onto the bed. She let out a giggle and began to take her clothes off showing both of us what we are about to have. We both let out a primal growl and took off our clothing. We then crawled on the bed. Rafael grabbed her and placed her on her hands and knees. He moved in front of her and placed his cock in her face. She gladly took it in her mouth, and he let out a moan. I smiled, I moved in back of her and slid my cock into that pussy of hers. It was so nice and wet too; I shoved all my cock into her. She gave out a moan which made Rafael grab her hair. I began to go in and out, taking my time. Letting her get use to my size, then I picked up the speed having

Rafael grip her hair even more. We are going to make this little Vamp slut scream our names until her voice goes dry.

I went faster and faster letting the motion of her bleed on to her giving my brother a blow. He loved it and had a fist full of hair, I felt her begin to cum, she moaned as she began to shake as her body was going crazy. We both chuckled, I didn't stop but went faster. Rafael had come just shortly after she did. I grabbed her hips and began to go different speeds. It drove her crazy as she began to grip the bed sheets.

"Yes! More, more!" she yelled out.

"More what? And what's my name?" I growled at her as I slowed down.

"I want more of you! Damon!" she screamed out breathless.

I smiled as I picked up speed and let out a growl as I could feel myself begin to cum. I pulled her hips closer to me as I blew my load into her which made her cum again. Her body began to shake again as I pulled out letting her body lay on the bed.

"Are you going to fuck her before she comes down on that or what?" I asked Rafael as he was sitting on his sofa after watching me fuck her.

"Yeah, I was waiting for you to get done," he told me as he got up and flipped her over as she was still shaking from me.

I let out a laugh and sat down watching him make her scream and beg for more. She surely didn't know what she got herself into. She wrapped her legs around him as he went faster and faster. I couldn't help but let out a smile as I saw she was screaming for more. When he was done, she was getting hoarse in her voice.

"I want both of you to fuck me at the same time. I love getting fucked in the ass," she tells us as we both licked our lips hearing what she said.

"You want to fuck her in the ass first?" Rafael asked.

"Fucking right I do," I told him as I grabbed her.

I placed her on her hands and knees with her ass in the air. I slid in nice and easy, I let her get used to it for a few seconds. She began to wiggle so I placed my left hand on her hip and my right hand I grabbed her hair. I then slammed the rest of my cock in her ass causing her to let out a scream.

"That's what you get for being impatient," I growled into her ear.

I went back and forth slowly letting her moan and beg for a faster speed. I gave Rafael a nod letting him know that he could join in. As he did, I got a picture of Anabella looking at me horrified. I froze, I couldn't do any more, I pulled out and got off the bed.

"Damon, you, okay?" I heard Rafael ask.

"I'm not sure, I need air. Keep going she's yours." I told him as I grabbed my cloths and somehow walked into my room.

Anabella was still there looking at me with so much hurt in her eyes, like I cheated on her. The crazy thing is that it felt like I cheated on her. I walked into the bathroom and turned on the shower to get that vampire's scent off of me. I had to get her scent off of me, it was making me sick, which that never happens to me. I didn't care what the water temperature was, I walked in and let the water cover my body. I then washed up and let the scent of my soap fill my nose. I felt better, but want I really wanted was Anabella's scent all over me. I needed to fill my nose with her scent.

I grabbed a towel and wrapped it over my waist. I walked over to the closet and grabbed a pair of boxers. I slipped them on and walked out the balcony door. I opened it up and stepped outside. The cold mist of the rainy air hitting my face felt great, it was what I needed. I still felt this pain in my chest that was not going away. I took a deep breath and let out slowly calming me down. I needed to find her and find her fast.

I knew this was not going to be easy trying to find her. I needed her more then she could ever imagine. I grabbed the balcony railing and closed my eyes as I kept seeing her face so upset at what I did to her. I wanted to tell her that I was sorry, and it didn't mean anything. It felt like I needed to tell her that I was hoping it was her. I needed to make sure she was okay and that she forgives me. I wanted to hold her, I wanted to press my lips on her forehead. I was getting pissed off at myself for what I did to her, but how could I have known that she could do that. What exactly did she do?

I needed to go see my mother, maybe she could make some sense of it. If she couldn't I'm sure that she could tell me who could. I walked back into my room and pulled out a pair of lounge pants from the closet. I pulled them on as I walked out of my room. I headed toward her reading room, if she was awake, she would be there. I took a deep breath as I got to the bottom of the stairs. As I walked up to her reading room,

I saw that her light was still on. I gave her door a light knock and waited until she lifted her head.

"Yes sweetheart," she said as she looked up and gave me a smile.

"May I come in?" I asked as I stood up straight.

"Of course, sweetie, what's going on?" she asked as she placed her book on the side table.

"Can a human contact us through the mind? At least I think she's human," I asked as I sat down next to her.

"No, only our mates can do that. Our mates are either vampires or shifters. Why do you ask? Is there someone who is trying to talk to you?" she asked reaching out to hold my hands.

"Well, I'm not sure if she is a shifter or a vampire. I meet her once and it was very brief and since then I keep seeing her in my head. Just now was very weird…" I told my mother not sure if I should go in depth with what just happened.

She seemed to have sensed I was holding something from her. "Tell me Damon. Where you doing something with your brother and a female?"

"Yes, as I was in the middle of something this girl that has been haunting me showed up. She looked like I was betraying her, like I was cheating on her. I felt her pain and heartbreak. I stopped and I felt sick to my stomach. I went to my room and felt so much better after I took a shower," I said as I looked down at my hands.

"I'm going to say this, you may have met your mate. To know for sure, you will need to go to see the oracle. She will be able to tell you what's going on."

"Where can I find her?" I needed to talk to her, maybe she could help find what family Anabella is in.

"She is in the city; her shop is in the middle of the market." She gave me a smile and gave my hand a squeeze.

I gave her a nod, I stood up and placed a kiss on my mother's cheek. I walked out the room and toward my room. I needed a shirt if I'm going into town. As I pulled a shirt on, I heard a knock on my door. I walked over to see my twin sister Victoria.

"I'm coming with you." she said very short.

"No. this is a private matter," I told her as I closed the door behind me.

"You need someone to make sure you don't do anything stupid." She let out a long sigh.

"Fine, but you keep everything you hear to yourself. Not very many know about this. I don't need father and the rest of everyone knowing about it," I told her as I let out a sigh.

She gave me a nod and followed me down the stairs. We made our way toward the garage. I walked to my car which was an Audi R8 matte black. I unlocked the car and got in. She slid in and gave me a smile.

"What?" I asked as I started the car.

"It's about a girl isn't?" she giggled.

"How do you know?" I looked at her sternly.

"I heard the conversation with mother," she said as she shrugged her shoulders.

I should have known that she would listen in. She may be my twin sister, but she is younger than me by ten minutes. She was always into what I was doing, she has blonde hair and fair skin. Her eyes are a beautiful sea green, she was also a few inches shorter than me, making her five feet and nine inches. She also has a different ability than I do. For her, she can make people think what she wants them to think, mind control is a powerful one.

I have black hair and bright blue eyes; I have tan skin that is covered in tattoos. I'm also six feet and three inches. I'm muscular and a better driver then her as well. I also can change the energy in the room to whatever I want it to be. I also like to be by myself, and I party way to fuckin' much. I also curse way to fuckin' much as well.

I pull out of the driveway and toward the town in our realm, it wasn't very far but I didn't want to walk over there. Anabella showed up again, this time she was confused and reaching to me. It looked like she was trying to call my name, but she didn't know what my name was. I let out a sigh and told her my name and where to find me. She looked like she couldn't hear me very well.

We got to the town, and I pulled into a parking lot. I turned off the car and she looked over at me to see that my face had a sad look to it. Victoria gave me a smile and rubbed my back like what she would do when we were little. I gave her a small smile. She gave me a nod and we head into the middle of the market. We were going to get to the bottom of this, hopefully.

As we walked through the market, I could still feel Anabella in the back of my mind. Victoria was buying things left and right, I couldn't help but laugh as I watch her place things in her big bag that she insisted on carrying. She said she was Christmas shopping and birthday presents as well. As we walked over to the oracle's shop, I felt a weird vibration that was fucking with my head badly. I shook my head as I was trying to get it out.

I opened the door to smell incenses burning, the notes of dragon's blood, white sage, and lavender. It relaxed my mind and my body; I walked over to the window and wrote my name on the clip board. I sat down and waited until she came up to the front. I closed my eyes and took in the smells as it seemed to relax Anabella too.

A few minutes later the oracle came up to the window and called my name. I got up and gave Victoria a nudge before following the oracle. I was led into a small room where the smell was strong and more calming. I sat down in a small red plush chair. Victoria sat down in a brown plush chair next to me. The oracle sat down in front of me and lit a few white unscented candles.

"Give me your hands, Prince," she told me as she reached out.

I reached out and placed my hands on top of hers and took a deep breath.

"Close your eyes and relax," she said as her voice sounded like a song.

I closed my eyes and took a deep breath. I could feel her trying to search in my head. I took another deep breath and felt her inside my head now. She began to search everything that was running through it. It felt weird that I didn't tell her why I was here.

I then saw Anabella again but this time she was younger maybe eight or so. She was playing with her dolls. It then went to where she was about fourteen and was crying from a breakup. I so badly wanted to wrap her in my arms. It was now today where she was twenty-three, she was crying again from a boy who broke it off with her. This time Luke was there, and I felt the needed to crush his fucking skull in, but I also knew that she would be okay with having him there, it wasn't his fault that I have very strong feelings of protecting her.

I had all these feelings that I wanted to kill every fucking person that hurt her, I wanted to wrap her up in my arms and lay with her until we both fell asleep. I wanted to grow old together in a human way. I wanted to kiss her forehead and tell her how much I wanted to be with her. Tell her that she was my whole world and that I would burn the whole world down if anyone fucked with her.

I have never felt like this with any female ever. This was an odd but amazing feeling. I took a deep breath to calm myself down, I knew that if I didn't, I would go on a fucking rampage and kill everyone that looked at me. I could feel the oracle begin to pull one thing up to the surface that I was desperately trying to keep down. That one was in fact the threesome I was having with my brother that I saw Anabella's face looking horrified and heartbroken. I let out an uncomfortable cough as she dug deeper into it.

"This needs to be done to find out how she could contact you in this way," she told me as I let out another one.

I nodded my head and suffered the feeling of betrayal and broken trust. I feltl like a piece of shit now looking at the situation again. I don't ever want to feel like this toward her. I looked at my face as I saw her looking at me, I had a look that I have never seen before in my life. I never wanted to see that look ever again. I felt the oracle begin to go into a different direction in my mind. I couldn't follow the path she was going.

All of a sudden, she pulls up a line that's called a mate line. It's what we have that helps us with finding a mate and communication with them. If you run into your mate, there will be a signature of that person in your mind. If you complete the mate bond, then the signature will be more out there for everyone to see. I couldn't help but wonder if meeting her at the party briefly had anything to do with what's going on.

"Did you meet her?" the oracle asked.

"At a party for a few seconds," I told her.

"You both are searching for each other, and you need to find her fast," she spoke.

“That’s why I am here. I have been looking in our records room, but I can’t find anything.” I gave out a defeated breath.

“Keep going, you are on the right path right now. Do not try to lay with any more women, it will only make things harder. She is a very powerful vampire who is yet to find out about her true self,” she told me as she let go of my hands.

I opened my eyes and looked at the oracle. She had a silent look on her face that said I needed to head back into that records room. She gave me a nod as she stood up. Victoria and I followed and walked out of the shop.

“Um…what was all that? Do you need me to help you with finding her? Do you even know her name?” she flooded me with questions that I knew I was going to hear.

“I need all the help I can get at this moment; can you ask Luke to help? I do know her name, her name is Anabella that’s all I know. I wish I fucking knew more about her. First, I need blood and lots of it, let's go feed." I gave her a wink that meant let's go kill.

She nodded her head and then smiled as we walked to the edge of town. I haven't killed anyone or anything in a long time. This is going to be so much fun. We found a few slaves that managed to escape some vampires. They had made a camp. We crept over to the edge of their camp and hid in the bushes as we watched them. I liked stalking my prey before I went in for the kill. As I looked over to Victoria, I saw that she was drooling over them, I couldn't help but chuckle.

I looked back to see that there were five of them sleeping, I smelled the air. They all smelled amazing, I locked on to the closet one. I pounced like a cat on top of him. I sank my fangs into his neck, he didn't even wake up as I began to drink him dry. When I couldn't hear his pulse, I let him go. I looked over to see my sister having sex with one as she feed on him. I shook my head and walked over to one of the females. I bent down next to her and sank my teeth into her wrist, she began to let out a small moan. I reached my hand into her pants. I found her cilt and I began to rub it in a circle as I tried to have her moan instead of scream out. I knew the oracle said not to have sex, but I need my kills to not make any noise. After I gave her an orgasm, I drained her body of blood.

As her wrist hit the ground, I was already on to the next one. This one was the last female, I dug my fangs into her neck, she didn't wake up. She let out a few moans here and there but was fast asleep making it a lot easier. She didn't take much to drain her body. I look up after to find Victoria was already on the last one which was a male who seemed to be enjoying her a lot. I got up and wiped the blood that was on my lips. I looked over again to see her giving him a small bite, looked like she was changing him. I gave her an odd look; she gave me a wink.

I gave them some space, I walked to the edge of the camp. My mind began to wander to Anabella. I took a deep breath as I saw her beautiful face and those bright blue eyes. Her brown hair was long and pulled up in a beautiful braid that went down her back. Her skin was warm like the sun hitting the sand on the beach. She was short, my guess is about five feet and four inches. Her smile seemed to stop me in my tracks as I was turning around to check on Victoria. It took my breath away.

"Damon where are you?" I heard her ask.

"I'm coming!" I yelled back.

I made my way back to the camp to see that Victoria was holding hands with the one she turned into a vampire.

"What's going on?" I asked her.

"Funny thing is, I found my mate," she said as she motioned toward the guy.

I used my speed and stood in front of him. "You hurt my sister, I will rip you apart. Let's get you fed," I told him.

I walked out of the camp and waited until I heard their footsteps. I ran off toward the water just out of town. I wanted to check his speed; I began to let him get ahead. I smelled blood lots of it actually. He darted off toward it. I cursed under my breath. I took off after him as I heard Victoria calling his name. I got to where the blood was coming from. It was a hunting accident that went south. I saw him feeding off the human that was bleeding out heavily. I couldn't help but let him feed off of the human. I walked over to the vampire that was bleeding out, I couldn't let him die.

I shoved my wrist in front of his face, "Drink," I told him.

He gave me a nod and sank his teeth into my wrist and began to drink. His wounds began to heal as he drank. I gave him a nod and he let go of my wrist and took a deep breath. I looked over to see Victoria was talking to her mate who I was yet to find out his name.

"Vi what is his name?" I called out to her as I motioned toward him.

"His name is Bronx," she called back.

I gave her a nod and helped the injured vamp up.

"Were do you live?" I asked him.

"I don't have a place." He mustered up some energy to reply back to me.

"You do now. You will be living in my castle. How long have you been a vampire?" I asked as I cocked my head to the side.

"About a month. Someone turned me and left me to figure it out on my own." He looked down.

"Well now you do. You will be in great hands with our family. That wasn't fair to you," I told him as I let out growl.

Someone is turning humans into vampires and leaving them to fend for themselves. I will definitely get to the bottom of this as well. I gave the others a nod and began walking back to the town. We needed some supplies for our two new vampires, I didn't care what the others may think about the stray vampire.

"What's your name by the way," I asked him as I helped him walk.

"It's Arlo, but you can call me Rlo." He gave me a smile.

I gave him a nod and then stopped just as we got to the towns entrance. We both looked back to see Vi and Bronx catching up to us. I walked over to a bench that was next to a shop. I had Arlo to sit and relax, he gladly sat down and took a deep breath. I looked around the market to see that the shops that we needed to go to where still open. I looked over to see that he gave me a nod to let me know that he was going to be okay where he was. I nodded back at him and walked to the first shop that was closest to me. I walked into a bedding shop, having Arlo join us in the mansion was a call for bedding. I picked up a light green sheet as that would be his color. It would go great with his green eyes. I grabbed a few other things that would match it in the shop as well.

I walked out to find Vi, Bronx and Arlo still sitting on the bench. I placed the bags next to them and went to the next shop. This time it was clothing, he looked to be about Rafael's size. I picked up a handful of clothes and shoes. Whatever he didn't fit someone at the house could wear. It didn't take me long to grab everything.

The last place that I needed to go was the jeweler shop. I needed to order Arlo and Bronx crest rings and Arlo slave's choker for when he gets one. It was going to be a little while until they came in, so I got them something temporary for now. Something that I needed was to get my ring fixed as the center of the jewel was getting lose. The jewel was fixed in no time at all.

I walked back and waved them to follow me back to the car. Vi grabbed the bags and helped Arlo get on his feet, she also helped him to the car. Vi and Bronx got in the back as Arlo got helped into the front seat. I put everything in the trunk and then made my way into the car. I started the car and began to head back to the house.

Chapter Five

As we pulled into the house, I got a weird feeling in my stomach. I looked back to see that Vi got the same feeling. I parked the car in front of the house and flew out the car. I was followed by the rest of them as I got to the stairs. As I looked around, I saw nothing that was out of the ordinary. Then I heard a scream, I rushed over to the sound as fast as I could. I didn't care what I was about to run into. As I got over there, I saw that my sisters were tied up with holy water soaked ropes. The ropes were burning their skin. I pulled out my knife that I always keep with me and cut the ropes off. I looked around to see that my brothers were tied up as well, I ran over and cut the ropes off of them, too.

"What the fuck happened? Where the hell are mother and father?" I asked trying to keep my head.

"They took them to the cave just on the out skirts of the land. They were saying something about the lost queen, and they were looking for you Damon," my sister Alizah said as she took a deep breath.

"Who are they?" I asked.

"They said that they were the lost kings' guards that they want his daughter for their own," she said as she looked down at her wrists.

"Stay here with them. Help them recover and show Arlo to his room," I said to Vi as I turned to leave.

She gave me a nod and I ran out and into the yard. I could feel the cold air starting to come as Fall was beginning. The cave that they probably were hiding in was the one that was close to the house, on the east side of it. As I began to creep toward it to see who they really were, I saw one of the vampires that guarded King Black. I wasn't sure what to expect as I got to the edge of the opening. I did hear voices talking though.

"He's looking for her."

"Why? He won't ever have a mate, he's too wild."

"Where has he looked is the real question?"

"He's said to spend a lot of time in the records room looking for her?"

"He doesn't even know her name. He can't get too far without a name."

I couldn't stand how they talked and thought that they could own Anabella in such a way. I was getting ready to get up and kill every one of them when she showed up in my head.

"Are you really going to kill them?" she asked.

"Yes, they want to get to you, and I can't let that happen. You mean so much to me," I told her.

"If you must but kill them quick and make it bloody. Place their body's where people can see. Make a statement like you always do." She gave me a sweet smile.

"For you, I will do anything my love." I gave her a smile back and she faded away.

I let out a growl, I knew that they heard it too. One of them walked outside and toward where I was crouched down at. With one swift move I grabbed him and tore a chuck out of his neck. He didn't have time to scream as I began to stab him over and over with the knife, I used to cut the ropes that they used to tie my brothers and sisters with. It soaked up the holy water which was great. I then grabbed a stake and pinned him on the side of the cave.

I then waited for another to walk by the entrance of the cave. I wasn't sure how many where in the cave, but I knew that I could kill every one of them. I also wanted to know who was behind this as well. I waited a few seconds before one came out and oddly enough started to walk toward me. This time I grabbed him and began to stab him, he did scream for about a second before I drove a stake through him and placed him next to the other one.

One by one I placed them up on the cave's outer wall. I pulled off their rings so they could burn as soon as the sun began to rise. I could hear someone talking to my mother and father in the cave as I took a step into it.

"Where is your son?"

"He went out, who knows when he will be back," my father said a bit pissed off.

"Well, I guess we will sit here until he comes. I guess you will have to look as I fuck the shit out of your wife." I heard my mother begin to whimper.

I could hear my father growl as he tried to pull against the ties he was in. I ran over to the voice to drive my knife into his fucking heart. As I got to where they were, I saw that it was King Graw. What the fuck did he want with Anabella?

"Why do you want her?" I asked as my temper began to flare.

"Oh, my dear boy. She is my queen." He smiled at me making me even more pissed off.

"She doesn't even know she's one of us!" I yelled as I could feel the heat of my anger coming out.

"Oh, I know, I was the one that banished her father. I knew that if I couldn't have one of his daughters no one could." He let out a laugh that would make the hairs of a human stand up.

I let out a growl so God damn loud that it bounced off the walls of the cave. I leaped on top of him and began to rip his throat out. Something inside of me told me to have him stand a trial. If everyone found him guilty then I would be the one killing him and staking him on top of the outside of this damn cave. I grabbed the ropes that were on the ground and tied his hands up. I saw that there was a bottle of holy water, I grabbed it and began to soak the rope in it. I heard sizzling has the holy water hit his skin.

I let him sit there as I cut my mother and father free. My father began to beat the crap out of him before my mother placed her hands on his arms. I gathered her clothes and place them in her hands. I grabbed the traitor of a king and brought him to his feet. When my mother was dressed, my father placed his right hand on the small of her back and we walked out of the cave and back to the house.

Chapter Six

I placed the king in the dungeons and called a meeting with the rest of the kings. I knew that the rest of them needed to know what was going on before I killed the son of a bitch. I needed to cool off before the meeting, I walked to the gardens. I needed her more then ever right now. I thought if I closed my eyes and called out to her, she may answer. To my joy she did.

"What is it, Damon?" her sweet voice asked calming down just as fast as I got heated.

"I need you. I thought maybe you would calm me down and I wouldn't do anything stupid," I told her as I took a seat on the bench.

"Find me. I'll send you where I will be soon. I have to go for now, you got this." She gave me a smile before leaving me with more questions.

Like what the hell does she mean she will send me where she will be? She knows I'm trying like fucking hell to find her. I took a deep breath and shook my head. She was driving me mad, and I haven't even mated with her yet. I can only imagine what she will do to me when we do the mate bond exchange. I stood up and took another deep breath. I made my way to the meeting room as I knew that all the kings were here already.

As I walked into the room I could hear whispers, like I was wrong to lock King Graw up and that I was making shit up.

Before I could say anything, my father stood up and said, "King Graw tied my children up and kidnapped myself and my wife. He tied me up and stripped my wife of her clothing. She was also tied up and was threatened with rape if we didn't tell him where my son was. He deserves death in my opinion."

Everyone went quiet, not sure what to say as they all looked around the room. I made my way to my seat. I knew that everyone was going to be shocked to find out that one of the most well know kings was a traitor to our kind.

"He was saying something like the lost king's daughter is his, and he was the reason he banished the lost king. Something about if he couldn't have any of his daughters no one could," I told everyone as I was trying to calm myself.

Everyone was silent, it was so quiet that you could hear a pin drop. I looked around the room to see shock on everyone's face. I couldn't help but feel anger, pity, and sadness all in one. I took a deep breath; I knew they knew something that had to do with everything that took placed.

"You all know something that I don't. I want to know what the fuck it is," I said as I looked around the room again.

"Yes, the lost king as everyone knows him as, was the first true king ever to be. His true name is Vlad Dracul," said King Black finally after a few minutes.

"Wait… you're telling me that the girl I have been searching for is the daughter of Sir Dracul?" I asked shocked that my mate was of Dracul blood.

They gave me a nod. Could she really be a human? That blood runs deep, she has to know something. Or even like things bloody when it comes to her human food. I needed to find her fast. Her fangs would have grown in by now. She has to have everything in. Having vampire blood like that just doesn't stay dormant for very long. She will soon want to know what the hell is wrong with her.

"You thought that throwing Sir Dracul and his family out to the mortal world was, okay? You just don't fucking do that to the king of all kings! He needs to be brought back and given his kingdom back. I have a feeling that King Graw was the one who killed that human that some other human caught on video," I growled trying my best not to blow up.

"I agree with you but the only contact he had was three years ago and it went cold. I still believe that he is still alive, but no one knows where he is," said King Hall.

"What the fuck do you mean that you lost contact with him?" I yelled out making everyone go quiet.

"He seemed to not call us to check in. The last thing we heard from him was that his daughter was going to a college close by. His daughter is about twenty-three or so," King Green said as he took a deep breath.

I needed to take a deep breath and I needed to process all of this. I ran my hands through my hair. What the hell? She's been at that college for at least three years. Why is she showing up now? What the hell is going on? Should I tell them what's really going with me?

"Son, what's going on?" my father asked me, he looked at me.

I took a deep breath before I spoke. "I believe she is my mate. She's been coming to me in dreams, and I see her when I'm awake. I can call her as well. I believe it was her subconscious reaching out to answer me. I've been going crazy trying to find her. I've been in the records room trying to find anything I can find on the family. But the records room is huge and is going to take forever to go through."

The room was so quiet after I told everyone what was really going on. There was a still air in the room. I looked around to see that there was no shock but instead there was understanding on their faces.

"Do you wish she was always with you? Do you wish her scent was all over you? Do you think about her 24\7?" my father asked me.

"Yes, all the time. I'm going insane." I ran my hands through my hair.

They all gave a nod as to say that she was in fact my mate. I needed to find her. I sat back in my seat as I didn't know what to do.

"Go to the middle of the records room and his information should be on the self and all the information should be there. Also, that notebook has everything in there to do with him," King Black said as he pointed at the notebook in my jacket.

I gave him a nod and said, "What should we do with King Graw?"

"Kill him," everyone said.

"Who will be killing him?" I asked.

"You should be the one to do it. You are being watched to see how you will act as King," my father said.

I gave him a nod and got up from my seat. I gave everyone a nod and walked out of the room. I make my way to the library, I could hear Rafael, Victoria, and Arlo walking behind me. I was going to kill the low life King right before the sun was to come up. I wanted to see and hear him burn and the sizzling of his skin, I will cover his body in holy water as well. I shook my head; I needed to focus on finding Anabella right now.

I walked in and went straight to the records room. I then went straight to the middle of the room. As I stopped, they caught up to me. I could tell that they wanted to help me find her as much as I want too.

"Rafael, you take that side, Vi you take that side as well on the opposite shelf. Arlo you will take the opposite side that I take on this side." I told them as I pointed to the shelves.

They all gave me a nod and went to work on finding the Dracul family. I looked through book after book but couldn't find anything on the family. I took a deep breath; they have to be here somewhere in the middle. I looked over at Rafael and Vi to see that they may have found something. I then looked over at Arlo to find that he found something as well. I walked over to the other side of my shelf to find a lot of stuff on them.

I pulled out a few books and walked over to the table that was in there. Soon the table was filled with books about the Dracul family. How we came to be and how the family broke off. I also learned that my family and the Dracul family are the only ones not related at all. Which was a bit confusing until I learned that there was another family that was created just like them but in a different area of time and place.

So, this is what I found out; Dracul was a baby born from a half demon, half witch, taking the powers of his mother and the thirst for blood from his demon father. My family was created the same way just a tad differently, my grandfather was born from a female demon and a male wizard. He was to have many children and many wives as he never settled down with one mate.

Vlad was the only one to have multiple mates. It is said that the demon was the one to cause him to do this. His last recorded mate was a witch named Maria, who they only had one child named Anabella. He had turned Maria into a vampire during the mate bond ritual. The bond that they had was the strongest ever, it is said that she was his true mate. It also mentions that she didn't die and is still alive. I was a bit confused, but something told me to check the notebook.

So, I pulled it out and opened it up. There was a greeting in it that was not there before. It read,

Good evening,

I am Maria Dracul. I am still alive and am happily living life with my husband Vlad Dracul. We do have a beautiful daughter that is beginning to know that something is different with her. We have not yet told her as there are questions we do not want brought up. I believe that you, future King Damon, will explain better than myself or my husband can. She is also questioning her dreams here lately and is daydreaming a lot as well. We believe that her inner self is called toward you. Please be patient with her as she is still finding her way. Also, please keep this notebook safe and do not tell anyone that I am alive. I have gone into hiding for a reason that I will tell you soon.

Oct. 31st, 2021

I looked around to see everyone was in shock by what we all read.

"So, are we more of the true royal like the Dracul's were or are?" Vi was the first to speak.

"I believe so, everyone else is born out of Dracul's line or through ours. It also sounds like I am mated to last true Dracul as well," I said as I looked down at the family tree of his.

"Does that mean you're the true king of all vampires because of your mate?" Arlo asked a very good question to which I did not have the answer to.

"I could not tell you. My father or King Black would know that one," I said as I myself was curious too.

I grabbed the family tree book and the notebook; I am definitely going to look more into it after I kill king Graw. We placed everything back on selves that we weren't going to need for later. We headed to my room to drop off the books and then made our way toward the back yard. I met my father outside and we headed off to the dungeons.

"Get up, it's time you get what you fucking deserve," I told King Graw as I got to his cell.

"Fuck off! You are not worthy of her!" he spat at me as he stood up.

"Funny because that is not what I was told and read," I growled out.

His eyes showed fear as I unlocked the cell door and grabbed him. I dragged him out to the yard. His feet dragged the ground, I didn't care if he wanted to be dragged out or not. Everyone began to whisper things that made him mad. They were glad that I was the one killing him. Some were saying that I was going to take my time, some were saying that I was going to make it bloody. Others thought that I was going to make his death quick.

Well, what I really did was this;I threw him on the ground and stripped him of his clothes. I let him sit there for a few moments before using my nails and leaving long and deep slashes all over him. He screamed out in pain from how deep I was going, but I didn't care to stop. He left my hand bloody which only left me smiling. I didn't stop there though, I ripped out his front part of his throat. His screams stopped but you could still see fear and pain in his eyes. He wasn't dead, it takes a lot to kill us. Two instant deaths for us are sunlight without a family crest and stake through the heart with holy water. I was getting to the instant slow death in a minute.

As blood began to pool out of him my satisfaction was growing. I grabbed him and walked him up to the cave where he took my father and mother to. The ones that helped were no longer there. The only thing you saw where bloody stakes. I grabbed the other stakes that were on the ground and staked him by the wrist.

I then poured holy water all over him. The last thing I did was pull his family crest ring off his fingerjust as the sun was coming up.

Everyone watched as the former king died a very painful death. I wanted to make a statement that said you will die if you betray my family.

Chapter Seven

My father gave me a pat on the shoulder and said, "Son, that is what a king should be. Feared but also respected as well, you are getting there." He gave me a smile before he left.

I knew what he meant by that; my father was a feared king that everyone wanted to be on his side. There were different creatures that asked for peace from my father that I didn't think would ask for. I watched him put the fear in everyone but my mother. She was his saving grace. She always calmed him down when he would get out of hand at times. I thought that I got my ways from my grandfather but in fact I got them from my father.

I looked around to see everyone with shock and pleasure on their faces. I was so proud of myself. King Graw's line died with him as he was never mated and never had any children. I felt a bit sorry for him that he was never happy, but he was a fucking ass and deserved everything that I did to him. I turned around and headed back to house. I have a family tree book that I need to look through and get to know more of.

I made my way into my room; I took a deep breath as I choose to shower to clear my head. Maybe a clear head would help with finding more about her. The more I know the more I can explain to her. I began to peel off my clothes as I made my way to the shower. I turned on the water and waited a few seconds before stepping in. I stood under it for a few minutes letting all my thoughts and actions I did recently go down the drain. I then lathered my loofa up with my body wash and began washing my body. I took a small palm full of shampoo in my hands and began to wash my hair.

When everything was all soaped up, I took a step back and into the water to rinse off. When the water ran clear without soap suds, I turned off the water and grabbed a towel. I ran it over my head to dry off my hair before running the towel across my body then I wrapped it over my lower half. I walked out the bathroom and into my closet. I pulled out a pair of boxers and sweatpants for bed. I pulled them on and made my way over to the bed.

As I got into bed, I pulled the family tree book closer to me. I saw that Vlad in fact had a lot of children. Some where my dad's age and Anabella was the youngest at twenty-three. As I looked everything over, I saw that his kids branched off and did their own thing. Anabella had a branch next to her name, I looked closer to see that it was my name barley visible. How could this be? I haven't mated with her or even met her besides that one time at the party. That was like super brief too.

I let out a sigh as I tried my best not to think about it too much. I flipped through the pages to find anything I could about Maria and Anabella. Something to tell me where Anabella was at. This was going to eat me alive if I didn't find her soon. As I got to the page of her mother Maria Dracul, there was so much that I had a chance to read through. It had her family and history of her witch family that was at least three pages long. I found that she came from a long line of powerful witches. I was on the fourth page of her information to find out that she was mated to Vlad when she was only twenty-six. She then had Anabella shortly after she was turned into a vampire. There was a brief mention of her death, but it was said that they couldn't find anything on her death. I studied that part of that page for a short while to see if I missed anything.

I took a deep breath and shook my head. I needed to get some sleep, but I also needed to keep going. I could feel my eyes get heavy as I tried to read the other pages. I could feel my body begin to beg for my rest. I didn't want to go to bed but I had been reading the same line for about twelve times. I let out a huff and moved the books on the opposite side of the bed. I moved the comforter open and got comfortable. I pulled it up and closed my eyes. I got swept into a dream, but this was something that I never had.

I got to a party; it was some frat party that was at the local college. I saw that was Luke there as well. I walked over to him and tried to ask him what was going on. I looked around and saw that everyone was blurry. I couldn't make anyone out, even Luke was blurry. I went deeper into the house and found my vision got worse. My hearing was worse, as well. I heard everything but it was muffled and was a buzz in the air. I shook my head to try to get everything back. I then saw her; she was the only thing that was clear in this fucking dream. I made my way to her, but I got to her, and she faded away.

I woke up more fucking confused then ever have from a fucking dream. This shit is just getting fucking weirder and weirder. I looked out the balcony door to see that it was mid-morning. I took a deep breath; I needed to get dressed and go feed. I grabbed a tank and a pair of basketball shorts. I didn't want to dress fancy just wanted to have an easy day. I also didn't want to feed off the feeders. I wanted blood but not from humans but from animals. I also saw something that wasn't threw my eyes.

I believed I was seeing through Anabella's eyes. I was seeing her out in the woods, she was staking a small deer. It was like her primal side came out and her human side was not there. I then saw her jump on top of it and sink her fangs into it. Her eyes flashed back from blue to red as she began to drain the deer. I felt the recharge of the blood hitting her. You see when you have blood for the first time your body feels like you're on a high. You then sleep for two days like you're in a coma. If she lives with a roommate that might freak them out.

I felt myself walk out toward the woods, I felt myself move out of our realm. I then smelled a beautiful scent. It was of rose, vanilla, and cloves. It stopped me in my tracks. It was the most heavenly smell that I have ever smelled. I looked around to see that there was a small human like shape running fast like a vampire. My guess was that it was Anabella, I called her name, but she kept running. I decided to run after her and try to talk to her. I kept running after her to the dorms, I slowed down as I saw more people.

"Slow down my dove, people will see you. You are running faster than humans," I thought to her.

She seemed to slow down as I began to talk to her. I smiled toward her, "Tell your roommate that you don't feel good and that you will be in your room. Go take a nap, you will thank me," I told her as I walked past her and out to the woods on the other side.

She walked into a dorm building and toward the elevators. I gave a smile and realized that I was still hungry. I walked around to find a lost human hiking, but I wasn't much into them. What I wanted was a large black bear, so I went off to sniff the air. I caught a scent of bear. I ran off toward it and jumped on top of it. We fought for a few minutes before I sank my teeth in it. As I drank the blood, I felt like I had a veil lifted. It was as if doing this was making me closer to her, which was weird.

It's been since I was a young child that I drank blood from an animal. This time was different, it was like I wanted more of it. I looked around to smell more bears. I felt something inside of me run toward the smell. It was like something inside of me wanted more bear's blood. I shook my head trying to not go but I couldn't help going toward the bears. There were two big male grizzlies fighting. My eye flashed red and I could feel my fangs begin to come out. I toke off and jumped on top of the larger one first. I sank my teeth into the side of its neck. It was too busy fighting the other bear to realize that I was on top of him. He went down like a sack of skulls.

I heard a roar, I looked up to see the smaller one was barreling toward me. I rolled to the left side. I got up and ran to it, I jumped on top but as I did, he swiped me away catching my side. I let out a growl, I took off toward him. I tackled him to the ground and sank my teeth into his front throat. He was still fighting until I drank all of the blood out of him. After I drained both of them, I felt full and ready for the rest of the day.

I needed to talk to someone about what's going on. I have been fucking confused since I woke up. I took another deep breath and sat on the ground for a few seconds before I headed back to the house. I hoped I could get through the portal because I had no idea how I walked through it earlier. I got up and made my way toward the house. It was a peaceful walk; I wasn't really feeling like running all the way back.

I got all the way to the edge of the woods and saw the edge began to shimmer. I reached in, to my surprise it didn't bounce back. The portal could be ttempermental at times. We normally carry a key that to a human would look like a garage clicker to open it up. I walked toward it and felt a pulse of electricity and buzz go through my body. I got through it and made it into the woods. I sat down to take a break; I felt my energy begin to drain. I couldn't breathe, I began to cough I looked up to see my mother's face. I then saw black; I heard my mother scream out my name before everything went black.

Chapter Eight

I woke up and looked around to see I was in the hospital ward. I went to sit up, but I felt I couldn't because I felt tugs on my arm. I looked down to find that I was tied to the bed. I let out an aggravated huff, the nurse looked up from her computer.

"Prince lay still, I will go get the doctor." She rushed over to make me lay back down.

I laid my head back on the hospital pillow. This shit is fucking stupid. I laid there for what felt like an hour, but it probably was about five minutes that the doctor showed up. I picked up my head to meet the doctor's gaze.

"How are you feeling?" he asked grabbing my left wrist.

"Doing fucking great. When can I get the fuck out of here?" I asked.

"Well yes, don't leave the house for two days. I just want you to come here for a check up until I feel comfortable that you won't faint on us again." He gave me a small smile.

I gave him a nod; I couldn't do much of anything else. I waited for the nurse to come untied me. She walked over and untied me; she gave me smile as she placed the ties on the bed. I sat back up and saw my legs were tied as well. I took a deep breath and untied my legs before I jumped out of the bed. Before I could move my mother was right at my side.

"Are you feeling better?" she asked.

"Yes, now let's go sit somewhere and have a glass of tea," I told her as I grabbed her hand.

We walked out of hospital ward and back into the main house. I moved her along the house to her reading room. I helped her sit in her chair, I sat down next to her and called for her tea to be made.

"Where did you run off to? I saw you run through the portal and then it took about two to three hours for you to come back. Then you walked through the portal, and you fainted," she told me as she grabbed my hands.

"I was seeing Anabella hunt; it was like I was doing it. I then felt like someone was controlling me. I found myself on the other side of the portal. I saw her attack a deer and drink the blood. I knew she would freak out her roommate, so I got in contact with her through her subconscious to tell her roommate she wasn't feeling good. Then I got a strange craving for bear blood, so I killed three of them. When I was done, I wanted to take my time walking back to the portal. When I got there, I stuck my hand in and I walked through it. That's when I saw black," I told her as it all began to pour out.

She looked at me, I waited for her to say something, anything. She took a deep breath and poured tea into my cup. I grabbed the teacup and took a sip from it.

"That's normal, but you need to mate soon. Things well get a lot more interesting the longer you both are apart," she told me as she took a sip of her tea.

"I'm trying to find her so I can, but something is keeping me from introducing myself to her," I told my mother feeling a little defeated.

"It's yourself, don't worry. Your father was like that but he finally got the courage to do it without second guessing himself. You will too." She giggled and took another sip of her tea.

Well, that made me feel fucking fantastic, no it did not. I shook my head and finished my cup of tea. I then got up and made my way toward my room. The book was still laying open on my bed. I opened my door to find that

Rafael, Victoria, Arlo and Bronx were in my room.

"What the fuck are you all doing in my room?" I asked closing my door.

"We want to help you find her. Chill the fuck out bro. Also, you scared the shit out of us," Rafael said as he grabbed the book from the bed.

I let out a deep breath, I could use the help to find anything about her. I walked over to the bed and sat down. I looked over at Victoria to see that she had a notebook in her lap. She must have been writing in it while I was out. I ran my fingers through my hair, and I reached over to see what she wrote. I found that she was getting a lot of things down. I looked over to see that Arlo had a book that I didn't have in here before.

"What is that?" I asked him as I pointed at the book.

"I found it in the records room, it was just poking out of the shelf. Here, take a look at it," he said as he passed the book to me.

I opened it to find Maria's dairy, the last entry was just of last night. She must have found an away to place this in the records room. I took a deep breath and flipped to the front. I scanned the pages to find what life was for them after they got kicked out. I was happy that they enjoyed it, it was rough at times, but they managed. Then I got to the last entry to find what happened leading up to the deer getting drained.

Apparently, Anabella had been acting weird for a few days. Like her temper was on edge. Anything would set her off, her eyes would change, and she was complaining that her teeth were hurting. She would be gone for days and not remember where she went or what happened. Maria was saying that Anabella wanted rare meat. She was craving blood. The day I ran into her started everything. It seemed to activate her vampire senses that seemed to be laying dormant. Then just a few minutes ago she went rogue. She had skipped classes and went straight into the woods. That's when I came into the picture, I ran into her that's where it stopped.

I didn't realize that I was reading it out loud. I looked up to see the look on their faces. They all had a shocked look on their face, I didn't know what else to say. I looked around the room to see that the sun was dropping down. I looked back down to see the notebook that I wrote in was opened up. I took a deep breath, I grabbed the notebook and pulled it closer to me. I saw that words were appearing on the pages like someone was writing on it. Which was strange, I wrote in it and the words seemed to disappear like the paper was soaking them up.

I looked up to see that they too where staring at the notebook. I looked back down to see that it filled a page.

Dear Prince Damon,

It looks like you found my old notebook that I gave to your father. I appreciate the words that you wrote while you were trying to find me. I have the twin to this notebook with me. If you ever need anything, write in this and I will do my best to get back to you. I have my hands full with my daughter Anabella at this moment. She has been a challenge to keep her from asking questions. She is a curious one that she is.

Thank you, Vlad Dracul

I didn't know what to say but to stare down the book. I was so confused that I didn't know what to do. I took a deep breath and I pulled out an unwritten notebook to work in. I began to jot down a few things that have been on my mind. It felt like I needed to write down what I was thinking and felt like I was having a veil lifted from me again.

"What are you doing?" Victora asked.

"Writing, it seems to work a lot," I told her.

"How is it going for you?" Rafael asked as he sat down on my sofa.

"How do you think it's going?" I looked up as I saw him with a half grin on his face.

He shrugged his shoulders and got more comfortable. I let out a breath and shook my head. My brother is the only one that can make me want to rip his throat out at times. I continued to write how I felt and what was going on with everything. I wrote done the struggles that I was having being future king and finding my mate.

The notebook seemed to soak up the words that I was writing but I didn't care. I knew some that was worthy of it would be able to read it. I looked up and saw that it was raining its ass off outside.

"Hey, Arlo, can you shut my balcony door?" I asked him.

"Sure, it's storming out. I've never seen it like this. How about you all?" he asked us as he shut the door.

The rest of us shook our heads no, it's a bit odd to have an unexpected storm just come out of nowhere. I wonder if mother and father might have an answer for that. I looked around to see that everyone was still looking for anything on where Anabella was. I couldn't help but smile, two of them just met me were helping me even though I can be a fucking asshole. I let out a chuckle there has to be something that they want after this.

I got up and said, "I'll be back, I have to find father and ask him a question."

They gave me a nod as I walked out the bedroom. I ran my hands through my hair nervously. I walked down the stairs and toward his office. I got to the door and gave it a knock. I didn't hear anything after a few minutes, so I reached for the door handle and opened the door. As I walked in, I saw that my father wasn't in but that he was doing some massive work on finding Vlad. I looked around amazed, I walked out and went toward the meeting room. As I got there, I didn't hear anything going on. I looked around trying to figure out where he could possibly be at. Then I thought that he could be in the greenhouse, I walked toward the back door. As I opened the door to the greenhouse, I saw him siting there next to the Hellebore flower.

"Father, is everything okay?" I asked as I sat down next to him.

"Not really, but what's the matter son?" he asked me as he gave me a small smile.

"It's better if I showed you something," I told him as I handed him the diary.

He opened it up and began to read Vlad's writing. He read what Vlad wrote to me and then I showed him Maria's diary as well. I knew that he would enjoy the diaries as he was trying to look for Vlad himself. His eyes widened as he took everything that he was reading in. He looked up and out the windows of the green house with his eyes began to water some.

"Are you okay?" I asked him, grabbing the diaries from him.

"Yes, they are just really good friends of mine," he told him as he wiped his eyes.

"Is he the reason for the weather?" I asked out of the blue.

"He very well could be doing this. He can affect the weather so I wouldn't be surprised if he is doing something." He shrugged his shoulders.

"I thought he was in the human realm? I was making a joke, the weather started after he sent me that message in the notebook." I looked at him in utter surprise.

"Well son, he may be in the human realm he is still powerful and is fully capable of reaching us. He seems to be trying to send us a message with the weather." My father looked at me and then outside at the storm.

I didn't realize how powerful and how far his powers go. Tonight, is going to be a lot fun if he is in fact trying to tell us something. I was hoping that I could sleep great tonight, with this massive storm. I sat next to my father for a few moments before going back to my room.

Chapter Nine

As I got up to my room, I saw that they were still in there. I let out a yawn and they all looked up. Victoria gave out a huff and grabbed Bronx's hand, they both walked out the room. I let out a chuckle as they headed toward her room. I looked back to see that Rafael and Arlo were staring at me.

"What?" I asked as I looked at them back and forth.

"What did father say?" Rafael asked as he looked at the books that were still in my hands.

"He was amazed by the content, and he also said that the storm could be Vlad. Also, he said that Vlad is fucking powerful as hell and that he can reach us from the human realm. Which is fucking crazy and awesome at the same fucking time. Also, I'm hoping that I can get some decent fucking sleep too." It came out like fucking vomit.

They both looked at me with a shocked look on their facese. I let out a deep breath and sat down on the bed. They both looked at one another before they walked over to my side.

"It makes sense though. With his daughter's fangs and craving of blood he must be trying to get back his kingdom." Arlo brought up a great point.

"It does but are we sure that he isn't in trouble or anything?." I asked aloud.

"Well get some sleep and we will work on that later when we all wake up," Rafael said as he opened the door.

I let out a huff and shook my head, I could feel my eyes getting heavy as I picked up the books that were on my bed. I placed all the books on the sofa. I then laid back down. My eyes were wide open for what felt like forever, just listening to the storm outside. Then my eyes began to close, and I was out cold. What I hoped would have been a peaceful sleep, was another dream about Anabella.

I was at a party but this time I was outside. It was a nice size courtyard that had a beautiful fountain that had the Greek goddess Ceto in the middle holding up the top part. I looked around to see that the people were still blurry like the last one. I took a deep breath and walked around finding anyone that wasn't blurry. There was a small hut that was more then likely the bar in the back of the yard. I made my way all the way over to get a drink and check out the people there. As I grabbed a beer, I couldn't see anything. My eyes began to hurt and sting like fucking hell. I rubbed them to find that only made the sting worse. "Fuck." I said as it took me by surprise as I opened them to find a person who looked a lot like Anabella. I walked over to see if I could get a closer look at her. As I got closer to the person only to find that she was blurry as well. Why the fuck is this happening? I looked around to see that almost everyone looked like her in fact. How am I supposed to find her when my dreams are not allowing me to? I took a giant sip of my beer before I walked around the area again. As I did, I finally made my way to the front by the fountain. I looked over to see that it was really her, Anabella was really standing by it. I walked over and as soon as I got to her, she turned around.

"It's about time you came for me," she said.

"Where are you right now?" I asked her as I reached out to her.

"At a party, can't you see? I have to get back inside, come quick," she said as she gave me a smile and walked toward the building to the right of her.

I tried to follow her it felt like I couldn't walk. It was like my feet were stuck on the ground. I looked all over to find that everything began to shimmer and shine. Then it began to fade away as I got pulled from the dream.

I woke up to find the sun was out and shining very brightly. What the fuck? It is fucking bright out. I let out a groan and rolled over and placed one of my pillows over my head. I then felt something was pulling me out of bed. I sat up, trying to find the source that was keeping me from falling back to sleep. To my disappointment I couldn't find what it was. I had a feeling that it was something inside of myself. I took a deep breath and made my way to the bathroom.

As I got dressed, I felt the need to walk the grounds of the garden. I made my way to the back door when I heard a noise coming from the kitchen. I walked my way over to see what it was. I found my sister Victoria and Bronx her mate cooking food together. I let out a smile at the scene in front of me. They were cute, I guess you can say. But who am I to say something like that when my mate keeps fucking with me?

I let out a sigh and walked my way to the gardens outside. I felt a pull toward the rosarium. It was a maze to get to the center of it, I took a deep breath and headed into it. My mother loved her roses which is why we had a rosarium, it had all kinds of roses even the rare ones. In the middle of it there was a fountain that was beautiful and a few benches around it for people to sit. As I got closer to the middle, I felt the pull getting stronger and stronger with every step I took.

As I got to the middle, I found a single rare rose in a vase in the middle of the fountain. It was solid black with just the edges of the petals were blood red. Like someone took a black rose and lightly dipped it in blood. I looked around to see that no one was there. I walked closer to see that there was a note card next to it. It read this.

Prince Damon,

Please accept this rose and hope you find it useful in the search of me. People are asking questions and I have no idea what is going on.

Your dove.

I placed the card in my pocket and picked up the rose and vase. I sat down on one of the benches and placed the rose next to me. I felt the need to talk out loud to it.

"You remember that I called you dove? Well people asking questions is common. You need to let me in so I can find you. Send me more then a rose to help me," I said into the air.

I really do hope that she will be happy when I find her. I also hope that she doesn't kill anyone until I find her. I hate cleaning up after something messy happens. I think this would be different, I would kill anyone who tries to mess with her. I want to burn the whole world down just to find her, but I have a feeling this is going to take a while more then I would like for. I got up and walked deeper into the garden. I needed a good walk alone around the grounds to clear my head. This might be what I needed or something that would bring on new ideas in or open myself up for new messages from her or her mother and father. Which might not be a bad idea. Finding her was on the top of my list, it was something that needed to be done so I could sleep better.

As I got out of the rosarium I heard my mother call my name and said something about Luke was there.

Chapter Ten

As I got back to the house, I heard my uncle ask my dad if I found her or not. My dad just said no and let it go. I felt a smile come over my lips, my father was the one who didn't feel like explaining the whole thing to my uncle who wasn't going to listen to it anyway. I walked into the dining hall to see that everyone was having dinner that Vi made a little while ago. I took my seat across from Luke and placed the vase with the rose in front of me. I let out a cough to which he looked up. I gave him a look that was asking him that I needed his help with something. He gave me a nod and went back to eating.

"Sweetheart, where did you get that rose from?" my mother asked me as I picked up my fork.

"When I went out to the rose garden, I found this in the middle on the fountain. It also had this note to it as well," I told my mother, as I slid the note toward her.

"Well, she is trying all she can to have you find her." My mother gave me a small smile.

I grabbed the note back and began to eat what was in front of me. The room was quiet as we all ate. I pushed my plate to the middle of the table and waited for the table to get cleaned off. I looked around to see that the desert was coming out of the kitchen. It looked so fucking good, it was a three-layer chocolate cake with raspberry jam in the middle of the layers. It had dark chocolate frosting covering it as well. It was making my mouth water so God damn bad. I waited as they came and brought me a piece. The cuts where huge, as it got placed in front of me, I waited for the rest to get theirs.

I took a piece and placed it in my mouth. It tasted so fucking good, chocolate cake was my favorite human food. I would go to the end of the earth for this food. I know right now you are probably laughing but its true. It didn't take me long to finish it and look at Luke who was just finishing up his slice.

I pushed the plate to the middle of the table and excused myself from the room. I headed to the library but this time I was looking for a book that she may have hinted at in the note. As I walked down the hall, I could hear Luke's footsteps behind me. A smile came across my face as I got closer to the library. I opened the door and walked in. I waited for Luke to follow before I closed the door, he walked in and just as I was closing the door, I heard a voice. I looked to see that it was Arlo and Rafael with him as well.

"What are you both doing here?" I asked.

"We wanted to help, and more eyes are better then two." Rafael shrugged his shoulders.

"Fine. Let's get this over with then," I told both of them before turning around.

I walked over to the table and pulled out the note again. I knew that there was a reference to a book in that note. I don't really read but I felt like there was a hidden message in it. I placed it on the table and let the guys read it. I even placed the rose on the table.

"What do you think it could possibly be from?" I asked the guys.

"Beauty and the Beast?" suggested Arlo.

"It could also be Sleeping Beauty," Rafael said.

"Or even, other fairytales that have roses in them," Luke said.

I let out a deep breath and we all split up in the library to set out to look out for those books. I went to look for Beauty and the Beast as the others went and looked for the others. I have no idea what this book looks like, but I needed to find it fast. It took us a few minutes to find all the books that could possibly be about roses. We all placed them all on table and began to look over them to find anything that it could be. I then found a few things in Beauty and the Beast and Sleeping Beauty.

I then found what I was looking for, in the beast the rose petals fall until he found Bell. In Sleeping Beauty, the prince fought the evil and through thorn bushes to Aurora. She wanted me to fight for her and raze the world for her. I took a deep breath; she knew how to get to me. I looked around to see that the boy's face had a weird look on their faces.

"What's wrong with you all?" I asked them.

"Well, she is a hopeless romantic and well let's face it. You're not, you both are not the same," Rafael said as he shrugged his shoulders.

"Well, I'm okay with that. She's mine and I won't let that get in the way of us being together." I let out a growl.

"Damon, there's something I have to tell you," Luke said.

"What is it?" I asked.

"Anabella and I have been on and off dating. She broke things off after that party and has been turning down guys left and right. I really think seeing you that night had awoken the vampire in her," he told me as he sat down in one of the chairs.

I gripped the table and felt my nails dig into it. I could feel the wood begin to crack. I let out a deep rumbling growl, I could feel my eyes begin to change. I wanted to rip Luke's throat out and insides.

"I think I need to go lay down and get some sleep before doing anything stupid," I said with all of my fucking will.

They nodded and I walked out the door. I could hear the footsteps behind me, but I didn't care at all. I got to the bedroom and took a deep breath before I opened the door. As I did, I took my clothes off as I made my way to the bathroom. I knew that they would be in my room when I got out of the shower. I shook my head as I turned on the shower.

I got done and wrapped the towel around my waist. I pulled on the clothes that I had on my bed that one of them pulled out for me. I looked around the room to see that they were in fact still there. I didn't care, I wanted to sleep and find my fucking mate. I'm getting fucking aggravated that she won't let me find her.

Chapter Eleven

I got in bed and laid down for the day. It didn't take long for the sleep to take me over. It was a nice one, but I still got pulled into the dream. This one, I got closer to her, and I touched her. Let me just tell you what went on in it.

I got pulled into a dream and saw her clear as day. She was beautiful, I stood there in the middle of the room. I smiled at her, and she gave me a small shy smile back. As I walked toward her, our hands brushed each other, and I felt a buzz and hum that went through us. I could tell that she felt too. I saw her eyes light up and I stopped to talk to her. I then heard my name being called.

"Hey Damon, you made it!" I heard Luke call out to me.

I looked up and gave him a nod. I looked back at to see that she went and sat with a group of jocks. She looked uncomfortable and out of place in that group. I looked to Victoria waving her hand my way. I shook my head and walked over to them.

"She's here, Vi can you ask her to come over?" I asked.

"No, you need to ask her." She gave me a wink.

I took a deep breath and walked over to her group, "Would you like to take a walk with me?" I asked her.

"Um, sure I would love too," she said as she took my hand.

Then I woke up as soon as she grabbed my hand. I sat up let out a growl, I looked around to see that everyone was still in the room. I let out a loud cough, they all began to wake up. I let out a laugh as they jumped awake.

"I need to tell you guys the dream I just had," I told them as I got out of bed.

I began to tell them all about the dream I was having. When I was done, they were all had shocked looks on their faces. I knew that I was going fucking insane, by trying to find her.

"Would you want to go to the party tomorrow?" Luke was the first one to speak.

"I would fucking love to go," I said as I moved to get dressed.

He gave me a smile and said, "What about you two?" he looked at the other two.

"Yes, it sounds like fun," they both said.

We got dressed and headed down the stairs toward the garage. As we got down the stairs, I saw that Victoria was waiting for us. She grabbed Bronx and they walked with us toward the cars. I walked over to Luke's car, Vi walked to hers. We all got in the accepted cars and headed toward the road.

"Where is this party at?" I asked as we crossed over the portal and on the main road.

"It's a frat party at one of the frat houses by the college," Luke said as we got closer to the school.

I looked back behind us to that Vi was right behind us. I looked out the window to try to calm me down. Yes, I'm a bit nervous meeting her. I looked at Arlo and Rafael in the backseat to see that Rafael was explain some things to Arlo.

"We're here," I then heard Luke say as he pulled up in the driveway.

We got out and headed toward the house, it was nice and big. I waited for the rest to get out of the cars. As they did, I lit up a cigarette. I took a long drag off of it before I headed toward the door. I felt a strange buzz go through my body. I let out a cough and shook my head as I took another drag from the cigarette. The buzz got louder and then there was a hum as I entered the house.

That shit was fucking aggravating, I couldn't help but grab a glass of whisky to calm my fucking nerves. I walked over to the guy serving drinks when the hum got really loud. When the line moved, I grabbed it. I turned around to see her, she was beautiful. I didn't know what to do but just stand there. Everything became more clearer then ever. Her scent flooded my nose, and I couldn't breathe anything but her.

I took a step forward to get out of line, but I couldn't go very far. I couldn't even look anywhere but her. My eyes watched as she looked around the room and talked to the group of people she came with. She then looked over at me as guys were trying to talk to her. She didn't even look at them as they called her name. Her eyes landed on mine; they were a beautiful blue shade. We looked at each other for what felt like a lifetime. I never wanted it to end, I wanted to have her all to myself. I wanted her in my fucking room and her fucking underneath me.

She moved forward but then stopped. I felt my feet begin to move as well, I seemed to have brushed her hand like in the dream. In like the dream we both felt the hum and buzz go through. We also felt a shock too. We both looked at each other and she looked shocked.

"Hey Damon, you came!" I heard a voice say.

I looked up to see it was a long-time friend. I gave him a wave and walked toward him.

TO BE CONTINUED...

About the Author

Anna lives in Louisiana with her husband and animals. When she's not writing, she likes to spend time with her family and friends. She also likes to read, draw, and ride her horse. The passion for writing started early for her, and she has finally decided it is time to chase her dreams.

Anna has recently joined Bayou Queen Publishing as one of their first signed authors, and soon there will be many more books from her for you to enjoy.

If you would like to keep up with Anna, you can follow her on her Facebook Page by going to https://www.facebook.com/Anna-G-Berry-Books-314983496118252/ . You can also join her readers group on Facebook, where you'll get early peeks at her upcoming books by joining Anna's Book Nook at https://www.facebook.com/groups/2437872593111036 . Other places you can follow Anna are on Twitter, at https://mobile.twitter.com/AnnaGBerry1 and on Instagram at https://www.instagram.com/anna_g_berry/ .